# FROM HUMBUG TO HUMBLE

a novel

# STEPHANIE VERNI

*Merry Christmas! 2021 Stephanie Verni*

ISBN 978-0-578-30899-9

Dedication...

This book is wholly dedicated to my family. Year after year since I was little, and now with grown children of my own, we have loved Ebenezer Scrooge. We have delighted in him and have often wondered and discussed the details and possibilities regarding Scrooge's transformation and redemption. Reading the original text and watching every adaptation of *A **Christmas Carol*** possible, we all feel intimately connected to this character, as if he has become a part of us.

Therefore, among these pages, I have endeavored to tell the rest of the story, with my sincere apologies to the great, masterful Charles Dickens. If nothing else, I hope Mr. Dickens might be amused by my attempt to fill in the blanks.


AND FOR...


Lovers of the kindness of the Christmas season everywhere.

~ S.V.

## Books by Stephanie Verni

Beneath the Mimosa Tree
Baseball Girl
Inn Significant
Little Milestones
The Postcard
Anna in Tuscany - A Novelette
From Humbug to Humble
The Letters in the Books - Coming Soon


Visit stephanieverni.com for more information

# FROM
# HUMBUG
# TO
# HUMBLE

a novel

## STEPHANIE
## VERNI

# Prologue

# Uncovering a Treasure

Three weeks before Christmas when my class is over, a few students stay behind to ask me questions about the final exam, and we discuss their upcoming projects. Afterward, I return to my office for a few minutes and gather my things. The department secretary tells me there's been a call from my builder, and that he has something to show me when I return home. She hands me the pink slip of paper with notes scribbled on it. Obviously, my curiosity is piqued. I grab my coat and begin the walk to the Underground.

Teaching at the university and in my mid-fifties, life has become routine. Monotonous even. My husband, George, and I have two children who attend two different colleges and live in the dormitories. Life changes when the kids are gone; you have more time on your hands. And despite my love of the townhouse, the absence of our children makes it feel bigger than it is. Why we've decided to renovate the downstairs, I'll never know.

The home has been in our family for a hundred and twenty years, and I wasn't about to let go of it now. Luckily, George understands—and after all these many years—is finally appreciating my love of nostalgia and family history.

I walk at a quick pace once I exit the Underground, heading home, wondering what is in store. When I turn the key and walk through the cloud of sawdust, I can hear the builders working. The place is in a bit of shambles, and the sound of the saw stops.

Raymond, the older crewmember, sees me, my briefcase still over my shoulder, as I step over some of the equipment.

"Hello, Raymond," I say.

"We found this, Amelia," Raymond, the older crewmember says, pointing toward the kitchen table.

"Where did you find this?" I ask, not knowing what it is.

"Between the walls of the kitchen and the study," he says.

The cover of the box, though faded, is etched with the words "Tim's collection," and nothing more. Gently, I peel back the top of the dusty box, afraid it might shred into pieces.

The leather-bound diaries are wrapped in an empty flour sack and stacked one on top of the other. They are made of brown leather and a good stock of paper, though the ink has faded a bit. Scrawled on the cover are the words I never thought I would read—never in all of my life—and it almost feels as if my heart stops beating for a moment.

"The Diaries of Ebenezer Scrooge," the two read, and the other is labeled "The Diary of Timothy Cratchit."

I stand there mesmerized, as I leaf through the journals, my mouth unable to close.

"Are you related to the old miser we've heard about?" Raymond asks me.

"Not to him, but to the little boy he helped get well, Tim Cratchit. He was my great-great grandfather."

Raymond is stunned. "Well, this may be a pot of gold for you, young lady. Good luck with that," he says, and they begin to collect their tools and prepare to leave.

I thank them profusely as they walk out the door.

Ever since I was a little girl and I learned the history of our family name and how it had been linked to an even more famous name, I've been curious. By trade, I'm an historical researcher. I relish in uncovering the past. Perhaps that's why I love teaching so much. I consider myself a lifelong learner and relay that to my students. "I'm with you on this academic journey," I tell them almost every day, and I confess that I'm always hungry to learn more—to be enlightened by something new.

I feel extremely fortunate that the journals were preserved away from the light, within the walls of the old townhouse that my father had owned. Two years ago when my father passed and we took possession of the townhouse, we hired an architect and decided to make changes to the existing structure. But I never expected to find anything as illuminating and profound as these diaries.

Call it destiny, serendipity, or divine providence, but I now believe that these journals have been yearning to be discovered, and perhaps by someone who has the ability to do something with them. I am so surprised and blessed to be the one who may be able to share the findings in a meaningful way. I feel like weeping with joy.

As was the case with Queen Victoria, who took great pains to record her life and kept a meticulous diary, I could see that Scrooge had done something similar. From the day Ebenezer Scrooge was set free of a life of negativity, glumness, and lack of faith living as a sour person, he became so filled with joy, that he wanted to remember each of his days and record how he had striven to make the world, for lack of a better term, a better place.

Therefore, two years after finding the box, along with an inordinate amount of detailed research, a retracing of the events, and a dissection of these remarkable journals, I've woven together the story as best I can. Ebenezer Scrooge and Timothy Cratchit wrote beautifully. The truth is, I've been so immersed in this research that I sometimes believe I can hear their voices as I read passage after passage.

Perhaps you've read the book, watched the film, or seen the play. The tale has been passed down from one generation to the next. You may wonder if that strange little human named Ebenezer Scrooge was capable of changing overnight from a curmudgeonly miser and all around cranky person to becoming one of the most beloved people this side of London.

Yes. It happened overnight.

Therefore, within the pages of this book, I have pieced together the stories that have been documented by both Scrooge and Tim in their own handwriting. As a scholar, I have painstakingly researched all that I could through artifacts and interviews done with countless others who have heard the stories through the years, passed down from one generation to the other.

Furthermore, in a world where it's often difficult to wrap our heads around the role that we all play in the betterment of society, I hope to share the evidence that transformative change can occur—that an individual has the capacity to make a uniquely positive impact on our communities, and sometimes even the world. We are the vessels through which good deeds can be done.

For what I believe you will come to understand, as I have had the pleasure of learning for myself, is that if a legendary, former curmudgeon has the capacity to change and leave a profound mark on generations, so do all of the rest of us.

*Amelia Cratchitt Shannon*
*Christmas* 1987

Stave One

## Scrooge Becomes A Good Uncle

Perhaps no one was as pleased by Scrooge's change in nature more than Fred, his nephew. Year after year, with the hope of helping his uncle find joy in the Christmas season, Fred had made the annual personal invitation to have Christmas dinner with his wife and friends. And year after year, Scrooge had turned him down. Moreover, it wasn't just a pleasant decline of an invitation. No! It was a hearty "NO!" that Scrooge had asserted time and again, with the additional "Bah Humbug!" thrown in for good measure.

Luckily, Fred never lost his sense of humour, and even enjoyed poking fun at his uncle, much to Scrooge's dismay.

As the story goes, prior to that Christmas Day when it all changed, Scrooge did not make himself merry at Christmas—nor at any other time of the year for that matter—as has been foretold to you. He was indeed the grumpiest of all grumps who ever lived.

Fred had desperately wanted to have a strong relationship with his uncle—his only relative on his late mother Fan's side. And from what Fred knows of his mother, she had adored her brother, which endeared him to his Uncle Ebenezer even more. Try as he might, Fred never seemed to make headway with Ebenezer, no matter how many pleasant offers of dinners or lunches he made year after year.

Therefore, on that eventful Christmas Day when Ebenezer showed up at the front door of Fred's home, as he and his wife were entertaining, Fred was at first shocked, and then delighted to see his uncle. A smile crept across Fred's face that did not wane until later that evening when he and his wife were getting ready for bed.

"I am still astonished by Uncle Ebenezer's change in demeanor," Fred said to his wife, relishing in his uncle's affable congeniality. "It's lovely and marvellous, and I hope it will last from this day forward."

"Dear Fred, I am quite sure that your uncle has had an incredible change of heart. Did you see how much he enjoyed the games! Why, he was having more fun than the rest of us put together! And he ate up that lunch as if he hadn't eaten in years!"

It was true. Ebenezer had not just eaten well and played the games that Fred and his wife had selected for the joyous occasion, but he had thrown himself into the festivities wholeheartedly. When Fred had seen his uncle laugh—belly laughing to the point of crying at the answer to one of the "Yes/No" questions in the game—Fred had been delighted by his uncle's earnestness to befriend all those who were dining with them to celebrate Christmas. By the end of evening, when Scrooge had excused himself to walk home, he had become friends with everyone there.

Fred continued to ponder this remarkable embrace of life until he drifted into a blissful sleep.

*

Forgiveness comes in many stages, and Ebenezer had been downright giddy at his chance to right his wrongs. He was through being the person that he was, embarrassed by it, and he told Fred as much when he visited him and his niece that very next Saturday for lunch.

"I thank you both for welcoming me back into your lives. God knows you didn't have to give me another chance after how poor of an uncle I have been to you both. I humbly ask you to forgive an old fool for the pain he has caused you and for the time I have wasted."

"Uncle Ebenezer," said Fred's wife, "we are just so grateful that you are here. Just look and see how happy you are making my Fred!"

Fred lifted his face from the bowl of soup that the housekeeper had brought them. It was a steaming hot bowl of bean and parsnip soup, and Ebenezer praised the cook for her efforts. After they chatted over the course of the lunch, and when his niece excused herself from the table, Ebenezer and Fred retired to the drawing room. Fred's cheerful nature was reflected in the colourful atmosphere of his house, the walls painted in yellows and greens and blues.

"You look at the world much as your dear mother did, Fred. You remind me of her so much. Perhaps losing my dear sister was more painful for me than I wished to admit. You have her kind disposition. Never lose that," Uncle Ebenezer said. "I miss her dearly."

"I don't wish to change my optimistic nature," Fred said. "But, let us not dwell on such sad things today. You are a happy man, Uncle Ebenezer, and no one more so than myself is thrilled to see you such a changed man."

"And a changed man I shall remain, Fred," Ebenezer promised.

*

Ebenezer kept that promise. In the following months and years, Fred and his uncle grew closer still, and the amount of time they spent together made up for much of the time that had been lost. Additionally, Fred's father, Lewis, who was just a few years older than Ebenezer and had been Fan's husband, had moved back to London from up north. Ebenezer looked forward to reuniting with his brother-in-law, as they had grown apart when he moved away after Fan's death. Fred, of course, hoped Ebenezer and his father would become the best of friends.

As they sat in the drawing room one late afternoon, Fred said, "You will be surprised to know, Uncle Ebenezer, that babies are on the way."

"Fred, did you just say 'babies,' as in more than one?" Ebenezer asked. "If for nothing else, my occupation at the counting house has left me able to deduce that you are in for more than one baby?"

"Yes, at least it appears that way. The doctor believes he hears two heartbeats. Gracious! How will we manage two little beings at our age!"

"You will because you are able and kind, and your children will have the best mother and father two children could ever want! I am so happy for you, Fred!"

"I will remind you of this when you hear two babies crying at the same time!" Fred said.

Ebenezer laughed. Fred and his wife were in their early thirties, but the announcement of babies on the way felt heaven-sent to Uncle Ebenezer, as he knew how much Fred and his wife had wanted to have children. He thought of how pleased Fan would be to know that her only son would soon have a family of his own.

When Fred's father, Lewis, arrived, both he and

Scrooge doted on those two children—bless them! And while Lewis was the paternal grandfather, Scrooge became grandfatherly as well, spoiling the twins in every fashion he could. Right after the twins were born, Ebenezer decided to move from his residence—the one with the door knocker that turned into Marley's face on The Night (of course, Ebenezer took the door knocker with him to his new residence)—to a location only two streets away from Fred and his niece. He was determined not to waste any more time away from his immediate family.

"I've decided to host a party in your honour, Fred," Uncle Ebenezer said, "to celebrate your birthday."

"In my honour? Lordy, Uncle, what have I done to deserve this?"

"First, by just being you and bringing me happiness, and second, in all of my life, I have never thrown a party. I think it's about time, don't you? You must teach me how."

"I'm afraid that's all my wife's doing. She's splendid at it!"

Fred couldn't have been more pleased. Despite having twins, Fred's wife had more energy than any woman Ebenezer had ever seen before. She made it her mission to help Ebenezer create a menu to serve his guests and pick the right wine to serve. His new home, a tall house with an abundance of windows and flower boxes and an outdoor garden (because Ebenezer had fallen in love with bright flowers and colourful things after his experience with the Ghosts), was readied for an evening of fun. He'd even bought himself a piano. Imagine that! An instrument that he could not play, but was determined to learn how to play, and he had it positioned in the corner of the drawing room. Scrooge even made his way to the barber earlier that afternoon to have his hair coiffed, and he had picked up a new suit from the tailor; he couldn't remember the last time he had been fitted for clothing.

"That looks rather stylish, Uncle," Fred had said at the tailor's shop.

"Are you sure, Fred? It feels rather silly, if you ask me."

"It is all the fashion. You look like someone who is ready to host the best party in town," Fred mused. He was good at pumping up his uncle, who was still getting used to the thought of being happy.

That evening, many people who used to fear Scrooge and were concerned for his welfare, showed up as invited guests to his party. Ebenezer was a courteous gentleman, checking on his friends throughout the party. In attendance were Bob Cratchit and his family, and even little Tiny Tim, who seemed to be on the mend thanks to Uncle Ebenezer who had helped the family find the right doctor. The butcher, the toymaker, and the bankers were all there, too. Even Scrooge's previous neighbours had come because Scrooge had asked them to come.

Taking the plate from the server as she was passing the food around and urging her to join in the fun, Ebenezer walked around chatting with people; he looked, as Fred had said, at least ten years younger.

"It is amazing to see his youthfulness seeping out of his pores," Fred had said to Lewis.

"He is putting me to shame," Lewis retorted to his son. "I will have to start walking a bit more each day to keep up with the likes of him!"

When the guests entered the room, Susanna Fezziwig was entertaining the children. She was the granddaughter of Ebenezer's employer when he was a young man and had served as his apprentice. Wearing a bright pink dress with her golden hair pulled up high with ringlets framing her face, she scooped up the children and took them outside for a treasure hunt. A schoolteacher with a sweet demeanor, Susanna was so imaginative that Uncle Ebenezer followed her around, mesmerised by her ability to engage the children. He took mental notes of the way she interacted with them, treating them like smart, inventive, little people. Ebenezer remembered how he had felt that Christmas morning when he talked with the boy he now knew as Albert. He was the lad who bought the prize turkey for the Cratchit's from the butcher per Scrooge's insistence. Children were delightful, if only you tried to communicate with them, thought Ebenezer. They are enchanting, and Uncle Ebenezer felt obliged to Susanna for helping him organize the activities for the children.

The adults played a few games under the shade of the tree outside, for it was a bit hot that late July afternoon. He had provided enough fans for the women to cool their faces—and a few of the men used them, too. Nevertheless, at the end of the afternoon, Ebenezer was sad to see all his guests leave, including Fred, his wife, and the twins.

As he sat alone later that evening reading a new book that was given to him, he felt the stillness of the air, the momentary quiet of his new home, and he was aware of the sense of loneliness that overcame him. Ebenezer was genuinely enjoying being around people. Making friends and sharing time with others had improved his spirits, as well as his health.

When he would watch couples like Fred and his wife together, there was not a pang of jealousy that he hadn't a companion, but rather more of a melancholy loss that nagged at his heart.

He remembered the years he spent with Isabelle. The way her hands felt, the twinkle in her eye, and the way she made him laugh. What a fool he had been to admire money more than his own betrothed! Damn fool, thought Ebenezer.

Indeed, it had been many, many years since he'd had a companion—someone to love—and he had loved Isabelle. Yes, he had. The Spirit had shown him the error of his ways, and his regret mounted. Still, he couldn't help but wonder if it wasn't too late for him. The chance to change his ways had been a gift, and he was most thankful for it. So thankful, in fact, that he felt he could not ask for anything else, let alone wish for a companion, or wish to feel romantic love again in his later years, for he had already been given a second chance at life.

Of all the lessons learned through the Spirits, greed was a thing of the past for him.

*

Ebenezer knocked on the door, and Fred answered it.

"Good afternoon, Uncle," Fred said.

"Good afternoon, my dear Fred. Are the children ready?"

The four-year-old twins came bounding down the stairs, happy to see their Uncle Ebenezer.

"What have you brought us today?" little Magpie asked. (Her name was Margaret, but they nicknamed her Magpie for short. Ebenezer wondered if she would still love the name as she grew older).

"Yes, Uncle Ebenezer, what have you brought us?" her twin brother, Edward, asked.

The children had grown accustomed to Uncle Ebenezer spoiling them, but today, there would be something different.

"Well, children, today I come not bearing gifts, as you can see my hands are empty. But as it is Saturday and we all have the day off, I would very much like to take you to a bicycle exhibition that is taking place in Hyde Park. Does that sound like a lot of fun?"

The children's eyes widened, and Fred's face became illuminated.

"You do know what bicycles are, don't you?" Fred asked the children.

"Yes, but we've never really seen one," Edward said.

"Not a one!" Magpie said.

"Then it's a date. Let us go and see Queen Victoria and Albert's bicycle exhibition in the park!"

Fred, his wife, Ebenezer, Lewis, and the children made their way to Hyde Park that afternoon. The delight on Ebenezer's face as he watched the children marvel at the bicycles and at those who were riding them was worth everything to Fred. How far Ebenezer had come from the days of being glum and angry and full of bitterness.

As his children sat on the grass with their mother eating the picnic lunch they had packed, Fred asked Ebenezer a question that had been plaguing him since his turn-around four years ago.

"If you don't mind my asking, Uncle Ebenezer, were the Spirits real?"

"To me, they were, dear Fred. They sought my redemption, and I pledged to not let their efforts be in vain."

"I understand, and you seem to be keeping that promise, Uncle. But, did you actually see them?"

"I did."

"And you were not afraid?"

"Well, I never actually said that now, did I, Fred? They certainly scared me enough to never want to be the man I was."

And that was the first and last time Fred ever asked Ebenezer to tell him about the Spirits who visited him on Christmas Eve.

*

A few years later, when Fred's father became ill, it was Uncle Ebenezer who sought to help get him well, as he did with Tiny Tim. Lewis suffered a frightful flu—one that kept him in bed for nearly two weeks. Ebenezer, still a man of means with his business thriving, hired a nurse to be by Lewis's side during his sickness. She nursed him back to health, although there was a degree of uncertainty for several days as to whether or not he would pull through. Lewis had a fever that had spiked and scared them all. Ebenezer warned Fred not to visit, for fear of giving it to the children, and promised him that he and the nurse would get him well.

A few weeks later, still wobbly and a bit weakened from the illness but no longer contagious, Lewis was brought to Fred's house by carriage. Lewis stepped out of the buggy gingerly, holding a cane, as Ebenezer and Fred guided him into Fred's home. The children had made him homemade cards and gifts and he sat and chatted with them all afternoon.

"You have brought my father back to life, Uncle

Ebenezer. I am ever so grateful," Fred said.

"Well, it's the least I could do, Fred. You all have brought me back to life. The gratitude is mutual."

\*

One afternoon, as Ebenezer was sitting in his counting house doing what people in counting houses do, Fred's wife knocked and entered through the door. She was dressed in her favourite yellow dress. Bob Cratchit was sitting adjacent to Uncle Ebenezer, and the two were having a congenial conversation when they heard her enter. Their conversation was rather jovial in nature, and they bid her welcome.

"Oh, good afternoon, my dear niece," Ebenezer said, as he rose to greet her.

"Uncle," she said, planting a kiss on his cheek. Ebenezer blushed. It was not often that a woman of beauty kissed him. In fact, it had been quite a long time.

"I was wondering if you would like to help me with something I'd like to do for Fred," she said, her eyes mischievous in nature. Ebenezer enjoyed joining in on good fun these days; it set him in the right frame of mind. He'd become engrossed in the everyday joy of life. It was remarkable to see his changed nature, thought Fred's wife, and she delighted in roping him into all types of shenanigans. They had grown quite fond of each other over the years.

"Well," she began, and turned to Bob, "and don't you go anywhere, because your family must be in on it, too."

Bob looked stunned for a moment, and then rubbed his hands together. "The Cratchit family is in on it, too! This must be quite a sensation!" he said.

"As you know, Fred and I will be married ten years this October. And with our little ones taking every ounce of our energy—you understand what I mean, right Uncle?—I would very much like to take Fred on a little trip to the country. It mustn't be talked about with Fred. I want this to be a surprise, and I'm hoping between the Cratchit children and you, Uncle Ebenezer, you will stay with Edward and Magpie while we are gone. I long to have my husband's full attention for a couple of days to celebrate."

Bob and Ebenezer looked at each other. They had never been asked to be party to such a wonderfully, deceptive plan with such good intentions.

"Do you think the children will miss you terribly?" Ebenezer asked.

"If you are around, I think not. They worship the ground you walk on."

Ebenezer chuckled. He had worked hard to develop close relationships with his grand-nephew and grand-niece. For all intents and purposes, the children considered both Lewis and Ebenezer as grandfathers.

"I am quite sure the Cratchit children will be obliged to help entertain them while you are away," Bob said.

"And, of course, I am happy to help as well, my dear. You and Fred go and have a lovely little trip, and I will stay at your home with the children."

"With the housekeeper and the cook, as well."

"Yes," Ebenezer said. "We will have a merry time, Magpie, Edward, and the Cratchit kids. Oh, goodness, what will we get up to?"

Bob smiled. "You don't want me to answer that

now, do you?"

Ebenezer's laugh had become quite contagious. He was giddy with delight at being asked to stay with the children in his nephew's absence. Why, maybe he could even coax Lewis into having a bit of fun with them, too, since he was feeling much better.

*

When Fred and his wife returned from their days away, they found two pleasantly exhausted men: Uncle Ebenezer and an equally tired father. Lewis's tight waistcoat had diminished slightly from keeping busy with the children. Ebenezer and Lewis had reunited, and Fred was delighted by their resumed relationship. Fred, of course, had enjoyed time away with his wife, but he was itching to see the children. When Edward and Magpie came running toward him, Fred dropped the suitcase and bent down to take them both in his arms.

"Father, father! We missed you so!" Magpie said.

Ebenezer watched the children and was happy for the love Fred and his wife had for each other and their family, including Lewis and himself. Sometimes Ebenezer was caught pinching his own skin—his own skin!—because he was so thankful for the time he had been granted to spend with them all. Tiny Tim, who was also at the house that day and was now thirteen years of age and getting healthier by the day, even joined in the celebration. Fred was as kind to the Cratchit children as he was to his own.

Scrooge wrote of the time he spent with Fred's children, stating: "*I fear that I have missed out on one of the great pleasures of life; spending it with someone and raising children together. I wonder, had the younger version of myself had any sense, I would have loved having children, which gives one endless pleasure and pride.*"

\*

When Ebenezer went to town with Fred one day, they encountered a rather disgruntled man. The man was outraged at the butcher's place of business, unable to purchase dinner for his family, as the portion he could afford was much too small.

"You have the audacity to charge this amount for this measly piece of meat?" the man said to the butcher.

"I am sorry, sir, but this is the size of the meat."

"Dastardly service, sir, if I must say so."

Ebenezer, with Fred by his side, was witness to the scene. He approached the man and intervened. "Sir, if I may be so bold to ask, how many people are you attempting to feed?"

"What business is it of yours?" the man said, becoming even further frustrated and enraged.

"It is the business of someone who would like to help," Ebenezer said.

"Help me?" the man said, his eyes wide.

"Yes. So do tell me how many people you are attempting to feed?"

"There are six of us."

Ebenezer approached the counter where the butcher stood. "Sir, if you please, cut meat for at least five suppers for this family." He offered the Sovereign to the butcher to pay for the meat.

"Yes, sir," the butcher said.

The butcher was familiar with Ebenezer, because Scrooge bought the turkey from him for the Cratchit's on the Christmas morning after he had seen the Ghosts.

"Please, give my best to your family, and enjoy this food."

"But how shall I ever pay you back?" asked the man, who had calmed and was stunned by the generosity of Ebenezer Scrooge.

"What is your occupation?" Ebenezer asked him.

"I have none at the moment."

"Good man," said Ebenezer, "you shall come and visit me early on Monday morning and we shall come up with a plan. I have an idea."

The man's eyes widened. Ebenezer could see how utterly shocked the man was, so he explained: "Sir, until not too long ago I had been a selfish and unpleasant man until I realised what I had become. And while I can't help everyone I meet, I can help many, as is my good fortune of working very hard over the course of my fifty-four years, and I am desperate to do all the good I can."

"I feel so ashamed," the man said. "My desperation has caused me to be rude, and I must apologise to you," he said to the butcher. "And to you, thank you very much. My name is Daniel Worthsman, and I am obliged to you, kind sir."

"I had been quite rude most of my life, Daniel, so together, we will put that behind us. I will look forward to seeing you on Monday morning at Scrooge & Cratchit just on the square, hmm?"

The butcher handed Daniel the meat, all wrapped and ready to take to his family. He tipped his hat to all three of them and sauntered out the door.

"You have made that man's day," the butcher said.

"Faris," Ebenezer began, "what becomes of all the leftover food that you do not use at the end of the day?"

"Well, often we have to throw it away."

Fred looked at his Uncle Ebenezer as he scratched his head.

"The men on the docks—do they ever get fed?"

"Not that I'm aware," the butcher said. Fred looked unsure as well.

"You and I should consider a collaboration of sorts, Faris. Perhaps we could institute a means by which we could feed the labourers on the docks. Let us set up a time to meet and discuss this."

Fred looked on, feeling proud of his uncle once again, and believing with all his heart that indeed, change is possible, and miracles are real.

*

At Christmas that year, Uncle Ebenezer had tricks up his sleeve. He was determined not to let anyone in on it.

He had hired a man with a horse and carriage, and he had put aside the money to buy his dearest friends and family Christmas trees. They were all the rage—Queen Victoria herself had fashioned them exciting and beautiful, and Prince Albert had made them desirable. All over London, people were beginning to get into the Christmas spirit. A change had begun to take place, and Ebenezer planned to be a part of it. To make Christmas meaningful again.

He had also started going to church. Ebenezer found a parish that suited him. Sometimes Fred would join him, along with his wife and his children, but faithfully, he would attend services. He found great peace in it and scribed in his journal: *"I find so much solace sitting in the church by myself with my thoughts, praying for those I love, the people I have met along the way, and the citizens of London. When the Spirits shook me that eventful evening, as frightened as I was, there was also some strange comfort that came from it all. Well, except perhaps from the Ghost of Christmas Yet to Come. He was another frightening story, and yet now, I understand it was in my best interest."*

Ebenezer would find his pew. He would sing. That's right—he would sing! And though his tunes may have been a little off and out of sync with the choir, he sang because he was alive.

He rejoiced in that he had been redeemed. He recited the passages because he was not the man he was, and the glow and the light shone from his eyes, and the people who were with him on those Sundays felt his energy.

Many of them did not know the story, although little by little the story had trickled out. It had become a sense of folklore, which is why, dearest reader, this story must further come to pass.

For if we only know how it ended that Christmas Day with Scrooge rejoicing in the streets like an ecstatic maniac and know that he changed his ways, we also must understand the details of exactly *how* he changed his ways.

Stave Two

## Scrooge Betters Old London

Realising full well that he had not given as much as he had taken, Scrooge became intent on playing a meaningful role in society. The men who had asked him to give to the poor had become his closest confidants, and he'd forged relationships with them. Jeremy Given and Randolph Caris had been, at first, tepid to ask Scrooge for money. When he brushed them off cold-heartedly on Christmas Eve and then retracted his declaration of "Bah Humbug!" the very next day, he made a promise to connect with them.

The trio set out to have a meal one night in a local pub, whereby Scrooge had scribbled his notes on paper and was excited to discuss scores of possibilities with the gentlemen. The workhouses were overcrowded, and people were becoming ill. Treatment for ailments in London was below grade, and great improvements needed to be made.

"Gentlemen, I want to propose an idea to you," Scrooge said, after they ordered their food and drink and took some time to exchange pleasantries and discuss the week's events.

"Yes, of course, Mr. Scrooge," Given said.

"No, no, Jeremy. We will not have these formalities. How many times must I implore you to call me Ebenezer and I will call you by your Christian names. It is only fair," he said.

"Yes, of course, Ebenezer," Given said, correcting himself.

"What do you think about getting investors together to fund a new hospital on this side of the city? Perhaps even one dedicated to children. I dare say, it is much needed. Why, my own partner, Bob, has a son who could very much benefit from it."

"I believe that is a wonderful idea," Caris said, looking from Scrooge to Jeremy. "It would be such a benefit to the community."

"My thoughts exactly," Scrooge said. "As I am new to this sort of philanthropic work, what must we do to figure out who, where, when, and how much? I would very much like to put a significant portion of my money into it."

The two men were very good at this sort of thing, and they could hardly contain themselves. Given pulled a small notepad from his own jacket pocket and began to take notes, hearing Scrooge's wishes and desires to help improve the healthcare operations for this part of London. And it would be a hospital that had a universal acceptance of all humanity—all would be welcome—and Scrooge would not hear of it being put into place in any other way.

When the meeting ended, the two men agreed to find the very best successful Londoners to partner with him on this project. They also suggested housing the hospital in the abandoned warehouse several streets away from Scrooge & Cratchit as the best choice of location. "I am sure we could purchase that building and have it up and running within two years," they said.

"Will it take that long?" Scrooge asked, obviously wanting things to move faster than they may be able to move.

"I believe it might, Ebenezer, but we will do our best to move the project along."

You see, that's the funny thing about optimism. It's contagious. Scrooge wanted to expedite the project as soon as humanly possible, and the two men, feeling the excitement emanating from Ebenezer, wanted to help him see the project come to fruition.

Within four months, Ebenezer Scrooge, along with Jeremy Given and Randolph Caris, had secured two other well-meaning investors, and finalized the purchase of the building, hired builders and construction workers, and began recruiting doctors and nurses for the hospital.

One evening after closing up Scrooge & Cratchit, Ebenezer, who had tried to keep the secret under wraps from Bob, could no longer do so. The newspaper had plans to publish an article about the new hospital project, and Ebenezer decided he wanted Bob to hear it from him first.

"Bob, if I may ask a huge favor, would it be possible for you to take a little walk with me before you meet your family for supper?"

"Of course," Bob said, raising an eyebrow. He was wondering what his business partner had been up to the last few weeks, as Scrooge had silently disappeared mid-afternoon for undisclosed meetings.

They walked down the cold street that night, the feel of autumn rolling in full force, as the leaves turned colors and people slipped into their coats. Scrooge was chatty and he talked to Bob about all sorts of matters, for their relationship had changed from employer and em-ployee to one of friendship and partnership. He inquired about Tiny Tim's health, and when they arrived at the warehouse, they could see the building was already in the process of being transformed.

"Do you know what this is, Bob?" Scrooge asked him, looking Bob in the eye and wanting to see his reac-tion—earnestly wanting to see his reaction.

"An abandoned building?"

"Yes, that is correct, Bob. And do you know what this building is going to become?"

"Our new offices?"

"What in God's good name would we need offices this big for, Bob?" Scrooge chuckled. "No, indeed. This will not become our offices. Something even bigger—something even grander."

"I'm not sure," Bob said, scratching his head. "But I am anxious for you to tell me."

"This is going to become a new hospital, my dear man. It's going to become the T. Cratchit City Hospital. And do you know why?"

"You have named it after Tim!"

"Indeed."

Bob's eyes filled with tears. He had never in all his life heard of a gift such as this one. A gift that would continue to give and had the power to help many, many other people. He was absolutely speechless and was unable to form words.

"My dear, Bob. This is nothing to become tearful about, unless they are tears of joy. And I, myself, am feeling a bit overwhelmed by what has occurred, as well. After mentioning to Given and Caris my desire to create a new hospital, they scattered. They searched throughout the city and made inquiries until they found other investors, and soon after, work was being done to get this hospital in working order for our fellow citizens. I insisted the hospital be named for one Mr Timothy Cratchit, for without him, none of this would even have been a notion in my brain, you see."

"Yes, I see," Bob said. "And it was all your idea."

"It was."

Bob scratched his head and marveled at the site. And while Bob may have been a relatively simple man who revered God and family, there was a part of him that was a visionary. He had the capacity to envision people's lives being saved here.

"And now you have seen it for yourself. Imagine what this will look like a year from now and how doctors will be able to treat Tim and many others like him in order to get them well."

"Ebenezer, there are no words powerful enough to express my gratitude." Since Bob had become Scrooge's partner, they'd dropped the formalities of calling each other Mr Scrooge or Cratchit. They were on a first-named basis now.

"Then do not bother trying, Bob. Simply go home,

enjoy the company of your family, and share with them the news before the article is printed in the newspaper tomorrow."

"Yes. I will do that."

"And tell Tim I will see him tomorrow. I'd like to show him this for myself."

"I shall tell him," Bob said.

*

Tim wandered into Scrooge & Cratchit in the late afternoon, after he had finished his studies for the day. Ebenezer had installed a private tutor to teach the younger Cratchit children to read, write, and do their arithmetic. Tim was dressed in his trousers, a sweater, and a blazer, with a hat upon his head. He had a scarf wrapped tightly around his neck, and his eyes grew wide when he saw Ebenezer.

"Why, hello there, Tim! I'm pleased as punch to see you today," Ebenezer said.

"And I you!" Tim said, giving Ebenezer a hug. "Father told me about the hospital. He told me you are naming it after me."

"Well, it is true. I probably should have asked your permission first, but I thought you might enjoy the honour of having your name on a building, young sir."

"If it will help people, then yes. I am very excited to see what it will look like!"

"Yes. And we will get the best doctors to come and work there and help people just as Dr. Chiron has been helping you to get well. The change in you is miraculous, and you are growing taller every day. Why, you're almost as tall as your Uncle Ebenezer!"

Tim laughed. Scrooge loved to hear Tim laugh. On a scale of all things that pleased him most in life, Tim's laugh topped the list. It was a giggle, a chortle, a chuckle, and a snicker all rolled into one, and when Tim laughed hard, all those around him began to do the same. Laughter truly was the best medicine, and Scrooge regretted all the years that passed him by without a singular laugh in it. He wanted to beat himself up over the wasted time, but he didn't; instead, he stayed grounded in the present with an eye toward the future. He had many regrets, too many to name, and if he thought about them all day, he would have no time to enjoy the present. Ebenezer left as much behind him as possible.

Tim's pleasant disposition amazed Scrooge, and he truly enjoyed spending time with him. Bob was never jealous of Ebenezer's time with Tim. He readily shared Tim with all who loved him. But of course, Bob had many other children to keep him occupied, and while Scrooge was fond of all the Cratchit children, in Scrooge's heart, Tim would always be his favourite. Despite Scrooge's moniker of "Uncle Ebenezer," the two shared an intimate bond, as intimate as a grandson and a grandfather.

"Are you going to show me the hospital today?" Tim asked, as Ebenezer grabbed his coat off the rack.

"If it is agreeable with your father, I would very much like to take the walk with you that I took with your father last evening. And perhaps even treat you to a little something special over at the sweet shop."

"I'd like that very much indeed," Tim said, waving goodbye to his father, who would go home to his mother and his other siblings.

They began to walk down the street. It was a little warmer than the day before, and Ebenezer had closed up his place of business earlier than normal, something he'd been more inclined to do over the last couple of years. He marvelled at how fast Tim could talk, the way he saw the world and all its goodness, never allowing his illness to cloud or dampen his childlike enthusiasm. Ebenezer wondered if he had ever been like that as a child; his own father had been often unkind and blatantly cruel to him.

But Tim, he was a joy! He pointed to things and asked about them, wanting Scrooge to tell him all he knew about London, which as Scrooge came to find out, had been very little. He'd been too busy wrapped up in himself and his money so that he didn't enjoy the very place where he lived. This, Scrooge pledged, would change.

"I love that bookstore," Tim said, pointing at it across the street.

"We shall go and have a look," Ebenezer said.

Tim was a smart boy. He loved books, and Ebenezer was glad for it. His tutor had spent a great deal of time teaching him to read. Ebenezer wanted Tim to have as full a life as was humanly possible—to relish the things he, himself, had taken for granted. He'd been a fool for many years, and he planned not to waste one more second on such nonsense.

Tim pointed to a large encyclopedia looking book. It had a dark cover and was very heavy.

"Someday, I'm going to purchase this for myself," Tim said to Ebenezer.

"What is it?"

"It's a book about medicine."

"And why would you want a book about medicine, young Tim?"

"Someday, I'm going to be a doctor like Dr. Chiron. I'm going to make people well."

"Is that so?" Ebenezer asked him with a raised eyebrow.

"Yes," he said, matter-of-factly grinning at Scrooge.

"Then why wait? Let us start you on that road immediately. You are thirteen now. It's a good a time as any. You will work with your tutor to help you understand things you don't understand. There's no time to waste," said Scrooge.

Tim's eyes twinkled like the stars in a dark sky.

After they purchased the cumbersome book that

Tim was all too happy to carry (he told Ebenezer that he had just struck gold, getting this book, and that because his strength was returning, he could carry it), they continued on their walk to the site of the hospital.

When Tim saw the building, his eyes grew wide, and he beamed with delight.

"Oh, Uncle Ebenezer. You are doing a good thing here. I am going to work here one day. Yes! I am going to work here one day and fix people."

"I believe you will," Scrooge said. "I believe you will, young Tim."

The exterior of the grey warehouse needed fixing. Scrooge showed Tim around the outside of the place, and then knocked on the door. Several people were inside working on the premises, building walls and fixing the floors. It was a bit dusty. Tim was impressed with what had been done so far.

"Let's try our best not to make this place scary," Tim said to Ebenezer.

"Why on earth would we want to make a place scary? That is not our intention."

"I know, Uncle Ebenezer, but some children are

afraid of doctors. We have to make sure this place is not one that scares children."

Ebenezer understood right away what Tim was saying. He understood perfectly that Tim may have been—and perhaps still was—afraid of doctors. Of course he was; he'd been through a lot. And he also understood what he was requesting. If children were to be treated in a place such as this, it had to have just the right atmosphere so as to not frighten them. Scrooge made a mental note to talk with Jeremy and Randolph about this wonderful insight that came straight from a child's mouth—and a smart one at that.

"I will impart your wisdom, young Tim, and do my very best to make this place feel not at all scary for children," Ebenezer promised. When Ebenezer turned the corner, he was pleasantly surprised to see a familiar face.

"Daniel Worthsman! Why, it is so good to see you working here!" Daniel was the man Ebenezer had helped in the butcher's shop when he was down on his luck. He had helped him secure the job.

"It is good to be here, sir," Daniel said. "I have not forgotten your kindness, and I hear you are one of the donors making this place possible."

"Just as much as you are, my dear Daniel. Why, you have made tremendous strides here! Are you the foreman of the group?"

"I am."

"Well, it's remarkable, remarkable. This is Tim, my partner's son. He's thinking of becoming a doctor when he grows up," Ebenezer said to Daniel.

"Maybe you'll work here," Daniel said to Tim. "Would you like to meet Dr. Bellows? He is fine man and skilled doctor."

"There is a doctor here already?" Scrooge asked, amazed and pleased by this news.

"Yes. They are setting up a spot for the little ones."

"I'd like that very much," Ebenezer said. "We would love to meet him, wouldn't we, Tim?"

"Oh, yes!" Tim said.

Ebenezer patted Tim on the back, and Daniel led the way. Daniel showed them how much had been completed at the hospital, and they were delighted. There was a lightness in Ebenezer's step that he hadn't felt before. When Tim was able to briefly meet Dr. Bellows, they chatted for a moment. Ebenezer watched Tim study Dr. Bellows—he would become a doctor, most assuredly, Ebenezer thought. When they were finished seeing the progress on the children's area, Ebenezer and Tim said goodbye to Dr. Bellows and the workers, thanking them for their efforts.

On the way home, Ebenezer offered to carry the book for a while, seeing that Tim had carried it most of the way, both not complaining about its weight and not wanting to let it go. Finally, Tim relented after Ebenezer asked if he'd like him to carry it one more time, and when Ebenezer took the book from his hands and tucked it under his right arm, Tim slipped his right hand into Ebenezer's empty left hand, and they walked the remainder of the way just so.

*

Upon arriving back at the Cratchit's home, the house smelling of warm food and candles, Bob invited Ebenezer inside to see the family. Tim's face radiated with enthusiasm as he talked of the hospital and Dr. Bellows, the book Uncle Ebenezer bought him, and meeting Daniel.

"He took us all around—all around! We got to see the hospital being built, and I can't wait to see it when it's all done."

"Well, that sounds like a lovely way to spend your afternoon, Tim," Bob said.

"Indeed!" said Mrs Cratchit.

The children then gathered around and asked Tim all sorts of questions. Tim almost became breathless answering them all.

Just then, a woman appeared in the doorway, a woman Ebenezer had neither seen nor met previously. Luckily, he had already taken off his hat, so he bowed to the woman as Bob began the introduction.

"Ebenezer, this is Ms Cotterill. She is the tutor you so graciously finance."

"Lovely to make your acquaintance, Ms Cotterill. It was my understanding the children were working with Mrs Dane."

"Yes, Mrs Dane moved with her husband and children to Devonshire to take care of her ailing father. Ms

Cotterill is relatively new to us," Mrs Cratchit said.

Ebenezer studied Ms Cotterill for a moment because he found her so pleasing. She was of average height and slender, with a beaming smile and rosy cheeks. Ebenezer guessed her to be younger than himself, and when she spoke, her voice lilted and her eyes twinkled. Her rosy cheeks glowed with a perpetually happy expression.

"I am so happy to finally make your acquaintance, Mr Scrooge. Tim has told me so much about you these past two weeks."

"Let's hope he speaks highly of me, though he certainly has a right to tell the full story, right Bob?"

"Tim would never. He adores you, Ebenezer, and you two have become quite good friends."

"Oh yes," Ms Cotterill said, smiling. "He tells me only the good things."

Ebenezer was pretty sure he saw her wink when she said that. How lovely, he thought, a kind person with a good sense of humour. Since he'd seen the Ghosts, he felt lighter and more full of life than he had before, and in his mid-fifties (though some might have found him ancient), Ebenezer walked daily and took better care of himself.

Mrs Cratchit often made meals that Bob would bring to work to share with him. She worried Ebenezer was not eating as he should.

"Well, I wish to thank you for taking the time to educate this fine family of eager learners, right children?" Ebenezer said.

"You'll stay for supper, Ebenezer?" Mrs Cratchit asked.

"Well, I don't want to impose," Ebenezer said.

"You have become part of this family, Ebenezer. It is no imposition at all. We were expecting you to stay. You, too, Ms Cotterill."

Stave Three

## Scrooge Finds Love

Ebenezer found himself standing in front of a floral vendor. As he looked around the streets, everything seemed to lack vibrancy, and yet the floral vendor stood out like a Michelangelo painting. The colours vividly contrasted against the grey backdrop that was the city. He couldn't remember the last time he'd bought flowers for someone. Isabelle had been the last. He had loved her, but he let her slip away, his greed taking over for his heart.

"Sir?" the lady said, interrupting Ebenezer who was deep in thought.

"Yes, ah, yes. I'd like a little bundle of flowers."

"Would this bunch do?" she asked him. "Any particular colours?"

"Whichever colours you find most pleasing," he answered.

She assembled a collection into a small bouquet, and he paid her for the flowers. When he added another coin to thank her for her troubles, her eyes grew wide. "Why thank you, fine sir!"

He'd come a long way in the last couple of years, but sometimes the slightest thing like carrying a bouquet of flowers made him feel a little silly. But he was, indeed, giddy. He had asked Ms. Cotterill if she would like to take a stroll through Hyde Park with him, and she had agreed. They had been spending a lot of time together of late at the Cratchit home. This was the first time they would stroll alone, together. It was a beautiful Saturday morning. The trees had gained their leaves, and the warmer weather was upon them; flowers were starting to bloom, and the scent of spring was in the air.

He checked his pocket watch when he arrived, the park filled with families and people walking about, picnicking, and children running through the grass. Ebenezer could see Ms Cotterill hurrying across the lawn, making her way toward him.

"Good morning, Mr Scrooge," she said.

"Ms Cotterill, I am obliged to ask you if you would kindly call me by my given name, Ebenezer. It would make me feel so much happier."

"Yes, Ebenezer. I shall do that, but only if you will call me Katherine."

"It would be my pleasure, Katherine. And these are for you."

Katherine took the flowers from Ebenezer and smiled brightly, her eyes catching the glint of the sun that was peeking through the clouds.

"I am happy you agreed to walk with me," Ebenezer said. "I have been walking more, but not with company. It is nice to be able to talk with someone on a walk. I do love the solitude sometimes, but it can become rather lonely."

"Yes, it can," Katherine agreed.

"And where do you hail from, Katherine?"

"From here, London. My parents both passed, but I have a sister and a brother who live in the city. I live with my eldest sister and help with her boys, as well as teach and tutor."

"It is a noble profession," Ebenezer said. "And it does such good. Look at the work you are doing with the Cratchit children. Had I to do it all over again, I wonder if I would have made a different choice of profession."

"Yes, but look at the good you are doing with the hospital and how you have helped so many with your enterprises."

"Yes, my dear, but that is the struggle I still have. It came much too late. Imagine what I might have been able to accomplish had I not been so stingy all those years before."

"Let us not dwell on the past, Ebenezer. It gets us nowhere. We can only worry about the present and what is ahead. And I must say, I've been looking forward to spending some time with you all week to get to know you better."

Ebenezer felt elated. He hadn't heard such a compliment in quite some time. He couldn't imagine another human being so happy to spend time with him. He relished the kindness of Katherine, and the two walked for an hour that morning side by side, strolling through the gardens admiring the vibrant colours of the blossoms.

*

When Ebenezer thought about his relationship with Isabelle—the woman he loved and was intending to marry until his greed for money got in the way and he lost her—he'd never even thought about pursuing another relationship with someone else. He'd become so focused on his daily routine of work, work, work and money, money, money that love seemed completely unimportant. What a fool he had been!

How many times had his disposition stifled his ability to truly live? Realising the errors of his ways had been, at first, quite enlightening, but the ability to look back on one's life and see all the mistakes, the wrongs he had done, and his sourness and greed was often difficult to face. It takes an enormous amount of self-awareness to be able to see yourself for who you truly are. And it takes even more self-awareness to see all your faults, to recognise them, and then proceed to change—and to actually make the change.

Scrooge was definitely better for all of it. His least favourite word in the robust English language, he came to find out, was regret. He wondered how to navigate his future when he could still, at times, taste the regret.

And the loss of Isabelle—of love, of romance—was a true regret. For how is a person to live happily without experiencing some love in his life?

And yet, he had started to find love. He loved his nephew. He loved the Cratchit family; they had become like family to him. He adored Fred's wife, who had become like a daughter-in-law to him, and he was besotted with his grand-niece and nephew. He loved Bob. He loved his friendship with his brother-in-law Lewis. And yet at the heart of all of it, he was missing a companion. Someone with whom he could spend the rest of his days.

Isabelle had married a man and had a brood of children. He had learned that from the Ghost of Christmas Past. And quite honorably, Ebenezer was happy for her. She deserved to have adoring children and a supportive, caring husband. Ebenezer had not been of sound mind to provide that for her. He had jilted her in favor of wealth and was unable to commit to love as much as he committed to money. The very thought of it made him feel so ashamed now.

In his diary, Ebenezer had written: *"It haunts me that I caused pain for another, and I feel the need to apologise to Isabelle. She deserves an apology all these years later for my selfish behaviour. I fear she will not want to hear it, but I must summon the courage to do it, to ask for forgiveness."*

When he first met Katherine, admittedly, he was taken with her. She was kind and good-natured, and while she was ten years his junior, Ebenezer had no problems relating to her. She worked with the Cratchit children to help them learn; she was the perfect tutor. And, as Ebenezer was the benefactor for those sessions, he appreciated how good she was as a kind and dedicated teacher. The children were learning things he could only imagine learning. What a joy it was to watch the children blossom!

As well, Katherine was a good reader. She loved to read books, and she created a little library for the children. She would have conversations with them about the stories, about their content. She would work with them on their understanding of the tales, their merit, and their lessons. She also excelled at arithmetic. She was maternal, devoted, and Ebenezer could only imagine having a teacher as kind as she.

He'd grown quite fond of her quickly. They began to spend their afternoons together on the weekend. They would walk the gardens having long conversations about all sorts of interesting topics. They enjoyed the local tea rooms together. How long had he dismissed people and their insights regarding the ways of life?

"I cannot believe the stories the children have told me about your greedy nature. You are the kindest man I have ever known," she said to him one day, as they walked arm-in-arm through the busy streets.

"I wasn't always. You would have despised me had you known me before. Everybody did. And rightfully so!"

"I've never despised anyone in my life," she said.

"Well, you must trust me, my dear. I was far from likeable."

"But you are likeable now, and that's all that matters."

"I'm glad you think so. There were those I did not treat so well and they may have very strong feelings about my prior behavior. Some people are still afraid of me."

"I doubt that very much, Ebenezer. But it is irrelevant. We learn from our mistakes. We grow from them."

"What you say is true, Katherine, but I sometimes worry I won't be able to keep up this level of enthusiasm for the rest of my life," he said.

She stopped him from walking and turned to face him. Their relationship had become much more intimate over the last few months, and they could speak frankly with one another. However, at that moment, Katherine decided to take initiative. She had always been comfortable speaking her mind. Since Ebenezer had known her, she had been candid and had the ability to say what she meant. Why would she not do it now?

She took a deep breath, and then she spoke. "But that's why I'm here with you now. I'm willing to be your personal barometer of living well, with kindness at the forefront."

Ebenezer smiled at her. It was a genuine smile accompanied by a feeling of comfort that came over him. For the first time in twenty-five years, he felt as if he were not alone in the world.

He looked into her eyes as she looked at him. He felt like a young man, bursting with joy, admiring a beautiful woman's face, and the urge came over him to kiss her.

She noticed his hesitation and took a step forward. "You may kiss me, Ebenezer," she whispered.

*

Leaving work one day, Ebenezer walked in the opposite direction of his home. He wanted to walk in the direction of a possible chance encounter whereby he might be able to relay his sorrow and regret to the person who most deserved to hear from him. He'd tossed and turned all night, and he knew that the only way he could make the sleeplessness go away would be to meet the discomfort head on.

He walked along the streets slowly, hoping for a glimpse or a run in. When he finally reached the house—he remembered it distinctly from the Ghost of Christmas Past—he decided to wait outside, hoping he would see her.

When a wee child came upon him from behind, surprising him, he turned around in shock.

"Are you looking for someone, Mister?" the child asked.

"Indeed, I am. I am looking for an old friend of mine named Isabelle."

"That's my grandmother. Would you like me to get her for you?"

"If it's no imposition, that would be wonderful."

"I will tell her," the small child said, skipping toward the house.

Ebenezer watched to see what would happen. Would Isabelle come out of the door? Or, would she ignore the child's request? He waited patiently, watching for any movement from the house.

Hesitantly, Isabelle, with a shawl wrapped around her shoulders and her hair bellowing in the breeze, walked toward him. She was much changed since he last saw her. She was older—well, they were both older—and her hair was brown with shades of grey highlighting her face. Still, she retained a youthfulness about her, and her eyes were just as blue.

"Ebenezer?" she said as she approached him.

"Isabelle," he said.

"What on earth are you doing here?"

"It is quite a long story—much too long for a conversation at a fence—but suffice to say, I have come to offer my sincerest apologies to you for the treatment you endured. I was not in my right mind for so many years, Isabelle, and you bore the brunt of it. I am not sure if you can forgive me, but I at least wanted to offer the apology that you so rightly deserve."

Isabelle stood there, surprised, first by seeing Ebenezer standing before her after so many years, and equally surprised by his changed demeanor. Though time had marched on, standing there with her felt as if time had stood still.

"I am quite surprised by your visit."

"I'm sorry," Ebenezer said.

"No, don't be. I am surprised in a good way. I appreciate the words you have shared with me."

"I'm sorry it took me so long. This apology is too many years overdue."

"You look well," she said to him.

"And you," he replied. "Am I to assume you are quite happy here with your husband and your many children and grandchildren?"

"How did you know I have a lot of children?"

"Oh, just a guess, I suppose. Why else would you have such a big home if not for lots of wonderful children and grandchildren residing inside it?"

She laughed. Ebenezer caught a glimpse of the girl he once knew and felt remorse for the years he wasted.

"Well, in that case, yes. I am very happy. My children are wonderful. I spoil my grandchildren. I don't know what I would do without them, and my husband is a very doting man."

"I am happy for you, Isabelle. Truly I am. I beg your forgiveness for an old fool who didn't know what he had when he had it."

She looked at him endearingly, and they stood in silence, and the silence became a bit awkward for a moment. Both of them were lost in their thoughts, perhaps reflecting on what could have been.

"I forgive you, Ebenezer, and I am just so happy that you would seek me out to share your thoughts with me."

"I wish you nothing but the best, Isabelle. I wish

you, your husband, and your children the utmost happiness for the remainder of your lives."

He reached out for her hand, and she gave it. He kissed the top of it, a sign of friendship, remorse, and recognition of lost love. They both lingered for a moment, and then he bid her farewell. As he turned to walk away, he swallowed hard, acknowledging the melancholic feeling, accompanied by a little lump in his throat and a tear in his eye.

It had to be done, and so it was.

\*

When Ebenezer told Fred about how much time he'd been spending with Katherine Cotterill, Fred seemed pleased as punch, but took the opportunity to tease his uncle a little.

"Why Uncle. I dare say you are blushing!"

"Am I, Fred?" he waved him off, dismissing him so that he would not be embarrassed further.

"You are quite smitten, I see—besotted with the lovely Katherine." Fred patted him on the arm, and Ebenezer laughed. "I have seen her so many times with the Cratchit children. She is so very kind to Tim. How delightful for you, Uncle! I assume she has affections for you, as well."

"I believe she does, though I can't imagine why."

"Don't be silly. You have much to offer and you two seem to be excellent companions."

"I am hoping that is true, Fred. And, I would like for us all to spend time together," Scrooge said.

Fred loved how easy it had become over the years to have conversations like this with his uncle.

"Let's throw a dinner party!" Fred exclaimed, hoping his uncle would say yes to this, because ever since that Christmas Day, Ebenezer Scrooge had started to say yes to many, many things he had previously declined.

"Well, if you insist," Ebenezer said. "I would not say no."

It was as good as a "yes" in Fred's eyes, and he was pleased as punch to host a party so that they all could get to know Katherine Cotterill better.

*

On the day of the party, as Ebenezer and Bob had planned to close their business at two o'clock that Friday afternoon, there was a knock at the door at eleven.

"Yes, yes, come in," Ebenezer shouted toward the door.

It was Mrs Cratchit, and she did not look well. Bob saw it, too.

"Yes, my dear. Come in and have a seat," Bob said.

Mrs Cratchit was collecting herself, and Bob wrapped his arms around her. "Tim is ill again," she said, despondent. "He is not himself. His condition is scaring me. Ms Cotterill is with him now so I could come and tell you. Oh, what shall we do?"

Bob looked at Ebenezer, and Ebenezer looked back at Bob.

"We shall ask the doctors at the hospital," Ebenezer said. "They will set him right again."

"But it's not yet open," Bob said.

"You may be right, Bob, but there are a couple of doctors who are working towards establishing a temporary place to help children now. Go to Tim and I will find Dr. Bellows. He will know what to do."

Ebenezer grabbed his hat and wrapped his scarf around him. Like a lightning bolt, in a flash he was out the door, facing cold and blustery conditions; London hadn't seen sunlight in eight full days.

He trudged through the London streets with a sense of urgency and purpose. He knew what his purpose was now. As he walked past people, horses, and carts, he was on a mission: He needed to make a little boy well. He would do everything he could to help Timothy Cratchit; it had become one of his missions in life. Ebenezer took sturdy, confident strides. He could hear the rhythm of his shoes echoing in his ears. Strangely, the sound of his feet pounding the streets brought comfort to him.

A serious concern for Tim welled up within him, and he grew even more worried than he had been in years. Getting this child healthy again was his utmost priority, and it had magnified his desire to help as many children as possible. His own father had not been a kind and caring man. It still bewildered Ebenezer the cruel way in which his own father had treated him, and yet he also understood he might have gone down the same path had the Ghosts not rescued him. They say we are blind to our own faults. In the past, Ebenezer certainly had been blind to his own.

When he reached the hospital, Ebenezer was pleased to see its continued progress. He walked inside. It took only a moment for him to find Dr. William Bellows, working with a child and his parents. Dr. Bellows saw him, and he nodded to Ebenezer, understanding he was needed. He finished with his patient, then made his way toward Ebenezer.

"I'm awfully sorry to interrupt, Dr. Bellows, but I am deeply concerned for my partner's son. He has taken a turn and we are not sure where to go or what to do at this point. His doctor is presently out of town, so if there's anything you can do—"

"You are Mister Scrooge, are you not?" the doctor asked.

"I am."

"We will help you. The clinic downstairs is not quite ready, but I will come to you. Where is the lad at present?"

"He's at his family's house—" and Ebenezer gave him the address. The doctor grabbed his medical bag and headed with Scrooge out the door. "You will ride with me in the carriage, Mr Scrooge," he said.

When they arrived at the Cratchit house, Mrs Cratchit swung open the door and hurried them inside. Ebenezer and Dr. Bellows were escorted to where Tim sat on a small bed looking peaked and drained, but the twinkle in his eye let Scrooge know he was glad he was there and that he appreciated that he brought Dr. Bellows along. Tim reminded Dr. Bellows that they had previously met.

"Of course! Who could forget such a fine young man?" Dr. Bellows said. Tim smiled.

"Hello, Uncle Ebenezer," Tim said to Scrooge. "I am quite sure I will be fine now."

Ebenezer's heart sank, but he felt warm and full at the same time. He had never heard sweeter words spoken. He had the same affection for Tim as Tim had for him. They would forever be bound by circumstances and compassion. And Ebenezer knew in his newly open and jocund heart that Tim—when he grows and is fully educated—would become one of the finest doctors the city of London has ever known. He was sure of it.

Mrs Cratchit came into the room with hot water. The doctor knelt next to Tim and listened to his heart, rubbed ointment on his chest, and looked at his airways. "If you don't mind, I'd like to work with Tim for a few moments privately, so we don't smother him as we do a treatment," he said. They all obliged and gingerly moved away so that the doctor could work with Tim. They gathered around the dining table and Mrs Cratchit began to get busy in the kitchen and offered everyone something to drink. Ms Cotterill, who had stayed with Tim for the duration, moved next to Ebenezer, seemingly worried and exhausted by the events of the day. She placed her hand in Ebenezer's quite naturally, as if they had been together their whole lives.

"Bob, all will be well. I have the utmost confidence in Dr. Bellows, just as I have in Dr. Chiron. When Chiron returns from visiting his family, we will inform him of the treatments. We may have to have the two doctors meet," Ebenezer said.

"I agree, Ebenezer. That is the best idea. And the whole incident makes me even more impatient for the hospital to open. It is much needed—even more so than I imagined. And I've imagined quite a lot," Bob said.

"I know you have, dear Bob. But you've done far more than one could have imagined. You have lived in a manner that shows great courage and faith in getting your son well. Believe that he will be well, Bob, and that he is in the very best of hands."

When Dr. Bellows left as the sun went down, Tim was tucked into his bed. Tim was feeling slightly better, but the treatment would continue in the morning, upon Dr. Bellows's arrival. Ebenezer had sent Bob's youngest children, Emma and Evan, to Fred's house to let him know what had happened and that they would have to cancel the gathering. Ebenezer wanted to stay with the Cratchits and Katherine as they waited for Tim to feel better.

Two hours later, a carriage arrived on the street outside the Cratchit's front door. Fred, his wife, Edward, Magpie, Lewis, Emma, and Evan, exited the carriage as the Cratchits, Ebenezer, and Katherine met them out front.

"What is all this, Fred?" Ebenezer asked.

Fred looked at his uncle. "Well, my dear uncle, if

the party isn't going to come to us, then we shall bring the party to you."

"What a delight!" Bob said, clasping his hands together and getting a little tearful. They all helped bring the food and drink—and even a few decorations—into the Cratchit home. And Tim, feeling much better than he had hours ago, was permitted to sit near the fireplace with a blanket wrapped around him, to be with the people who cared about him most in the world.

As for Ebenezer Scrooge, he marvelled at it all. He had planned to ask for Katherine's hand at the party (Fred was the only one who knew of it!), so the surprise of it stunned everyone there.

"If I might have a minute of your attention, I'd like to say a few words," Ebenezer said to his family and friends. They all quieted down from their chatter and turned to face him.

"Firstly, I'd like to thank Fred for this wonderful feast he has brought to us and for us. Always thoughtful, our Fred, especially in times of need. Secondly, I'd like to say how splendid it is to see Tim coming along so well. Let us raise our glasses to Fred and Tim." And so they did.

"Thirdly, I am not sure if this is the most opportune moment to ask this question, but as Katherine and I have found each other over these past several months and she has quite literally brought my heart back to life, it would henceforth be my dream, if you, Katherine Cotterill, would be my wife and share my life." Ebenezer had actually lowered himself to be situated on one knee, and Katherine, when hearing his heartfelt thoughts and expression and seeing the ring that he had bought for her, began to cry, as she reached to hug him and the room erupted with clapping and cheers.

She, of course, said "yes."

It was an emotional display of affection, and both Ebenezer and Katherine beamed with delight. Bob and Mrs Cratchit were thrilled for some happy news. This display of love, of course, lifted everyone's spirits for the rest of the evening and left them feeling incredibly happy. Before long, the sounds of inextricable joyfulness emanated from the Cratchit home.

Ebenezer took a moment to himself and looked around the room. Everyone he loved dearly was under one roof. With a quick glance up to the heavens, he silently gave thanks to those who set him straight. He had never dreamed such a level of contentment was possible in life. He had never before truly understood the notion of hope. More than ever before, he believed in the power of love, family, and friendship.

It meant everything to him now.

Stave Four

## Tim's Recollections

Tim was only seven when Ebenezer Scrooge was visited by the Ghosts. A mere child—and a frail one at that—Tim only knew Ebenezer from the stories his father would tell and from the occasional prior visits he paid to the office of Scrooge & Marley. Bob Cratchit was not a man to speak ill of anyone, even of those people with extremely unpleasant dispositions. Despite that Ebenezer Scrooge was a miserable miser and business owner, Bob needed to earn an income and provide for his family, and he endured much from Ebenezer in the days before their relationship turned for the better.

Tim's innocence and belief in people's capacity to do good even as a young child caused his mother, Mrs

Cratchit, to proclaim that Tim might have the makings of a vicar, for his goodness was inherent and his kindness contagious.

"Timothy Michael Cratchit — you may be one of the best people God has put on this very Earth," she had said one day, touched by the way he cared for his brothers and sisters. Of course, she was perpetually concerned for Tim's health, and the family had to work hard to keep Tim well.

Tim's family loved him—adored him. And Tim knew that, and it always sustained him, even during his most challenging days.

Which was quite the opposite of Ebenezer's father, who blamed his son for his beloved wife's death in childbirth. Ebenezer's father could barely look at him when he was young and held him in contempt. When Tim had grown and Ebenezer aged, he confessed to Tim one day during an honest conversation, something about his father. "My own father was not a loving man, so all that I do now, I do with the rigorous spirit and passion that I would have done had you been my own boy, Timothy," said Ebenezer.

When Ebenezer became involved in the Cratchit family's lives, it was immediate and lasting. Once he saw the error of his ways and set about correcting them, in Tim's mind, his Uncle Ebenezer never looked back. Helping the Cratchit family had become one of his most concentrated efforts. Bob was overwhelmed with gratitude for both the financial support and friendship Scrooge provided, but Tim sometimes thought his father felt awkward for allowing such charity.

Tim overheard a conversation with his parents, whereby his father said the following: "I don't want to seem ungrateful, because I know how incredibly generous he is being, but I don't know how to repay someone who gives this type of help."

"You don't worry about how to repay him, dearest," his mother had responded. "He doesn't look at it that way. It's not a debt. He wants to help our family. You just thank him profusely and we do all we can to offer him back the love that he has so generously offered us."

Tim remembered this as the turning point, when Ebenezer Scrooge became Uncle Ebenezer from that day forward to all the Cratchit children. And the Cratchits

embraced Fred and his family, as well. They all came together and genuinely enjoyed each other's company.

Perhaps it all began when Ebenezer became a
benefactor to the children and desperately wanted to
help them in their education and their futures. Not only
did Ebenezer Scrooge become giving of his money, but
he also became very giving of his time. The more time he
spent with them, the closer they all grew. Fred and his
wife and children also became part of the family, and before long, they were rarely apart for more than a week's
time.

Tim also noticed something miraculous happened
to Uncle Ebenezer. There was a certain glow about him.
Ebenezer Scrooge decided that he was going to have
a rich and full life with the years that remained to him,
however many years that would be. It was remarkable, really. Tim noticed that when you set your sights on something, what one thought was unattainable became quite
within your grasp. He learned something important from
seeing Ebenezer's tenacity.

The doctors did, of course, help Tim to get well
again. Dr. Chiron and Dr. Bellows were both brilliant

at their work, and the combination of the two doctors working together toward bettering Tim's health was welcome. Tim was incredibly grateful that Uncle Ebenezer had connected his family with the very best of the best. He could only imagine what it cost to pay those bills, but Ebenezer would never share those details. No, never, for you see, he enjoyed surprises more than anyone Tim had met! Ebenezer would never burden Tim's father with any of that information.

When Tim grew up, became stronger, and healed (yes, he did heal fully and well thanks to the great care he received!), he began to notice things. He realised how busy Ebenezer was with his various activities, but Tim never really knew the impact Uncle Ebenezer made until he was a much older boy. Ebenezer had become a reliable contributor to the people of London, and he went from a man who once lacked empathy to a man who ended up showing a great deal of compassion toward others.

He was intent on helping others quietly rather than leaving a big mark. Most of his endeavours, businesses, and programs he established, he did so discreetly and without fanfare. The choices Ebenezer Scrooge made in the end were done out of the goodness of his heart, and as he said to Tim one afternoon when he was nearly 20 years old, "I just hope to leave the world a little brighter than it was before I was reborn." And that he did.

With his beloved Katherine by his side, the pair attended fundraisers, gave money to various charities, and worked with other philanthropists and entrepreneurs to create new businesses to help the city thrive. She, too, worked tirelessly, and was particularly keen on establishing a school, which they eventually did open after a couple of years of work. Katherine kept her eyes on that project, obviously wanting it to succeed, which it did, and scores of children were able to learn in an environment that both valued them and gave them faith in themselves.

Tim was awestruck by the sheer number of projects Uncle Ebenezer had become involved with, from the school to the hospital to a reputable orphanage that kept children safe and happy until they were adopted.

"Do you know all the things Uncle Ebenezer is involved with, Father?" Tim asked Bob one rainy afternoon when they shared a bowl of soup together at a local pub.

"I do, Tim. He's done quite a lot."

"And that's why you have so much more responsibility at work now and had to hire Mr Wayson and Mr Cartwright?"

"It is. I'm fine. I love working with your Uncle Ebenezer at Scrooge & Cratchit, and he has taken to working hard for various causes, helping in any way he can."

"I love that about him," Tim said, the adoration he had for Ebenezer apparent.

"I've grown to love that about him, too," Bob said. "He's changed our lives. He's helped to get you well. He was instrumental in getting us our new home, and he has helped educate our family. His kindness is bound by no limits these days, whatsoever."

"And now, he's going to help me become a doctor. I don't know where I'd be without you, Mother, and Uncle Ebenezer. Thank you, Father, for all you've done for me."

Bob swallowed hard and fought back a tear. How was it possible to be the father of such a remarkable young man? No longer the little boy he was, Bob knew he would be the very best doctor London had ever seen.

He would be compassionate and caring, especially after all he'd been through with his own illness. Coupled with his intelligence and gentle, sunny disposition, Tim had all the qualities necessary to not only nurse people back to health and cure them, but to encourage them to hold onto hope. Bob beamed with pride as he looked at his son.

"I couldn't be prouder to call you my own, Mr Timothy Cratchit," Bob said.

*

Tim began writing in his journal sometime around the age of twelve or thirteen and continued writing in it through adulthood. He got the idea from Ebenezer, when he saw him writing in his own journals. When Tim asked him why he kept the journals, he simply said "to remember." Katherine had worked tirelessly with the children on their studies, and Tim had fallen in love with books and words. His journal became a place where he could explore his thoughts and feelings and keep them safe. In those writings, Tim explored his life as a Cratchit and his relationship with Ebenezer Scrooge.

As he grew older and busier, he began to write less, and yet the writing became much more analytical. One passage, in particular, notes his connection to Uncle Ebenezer, and the way he revered him.

*"While Uncle Ebenezer may not be a blood relative, and he may have found his way to us through Father and work and the Ghosts he references often, I believe he is a kindred spirit by every definition of the word. Uncle Ebenezer is the kindest, most thoughtful, engaged, and loving Uncle any of us could have wished for. Were it not for Uncle Ebenezer, I may not even be scribbling in this journal, and I certainly wouldn't be on the path of becoming a doctor, because I would most likely not be well enough to do so. Uncle Ebenezer helped us immeasurably on both of those counts,"* Tim wrote.

On another occasion, Tim referenced the way Uncle Ebenezer looked when Tim announced to the family that he had been accepted into the medical studies program. *"Uncle Ebenezer's eyes—I had never seen them look quite so—were filled with water, as he tried to bat away the tears of joy at my news. I was moved by how proud he was of me at that moment."*

*

When Tim became a doctor years later, and his sister Belinda became a nurse, the family celebrated. Mrs Cratchit hosted the biggest gathering in honour of both Tim and Belinda's accomplishments, and spent hours preparing the house. Not only were Fred and his family invited, along with Ebenezer, Katherine, and Lewis, but also neighbours and friends. The Cratchit children prepared a humourous short skit they performed, and Belinda played the piano.

Tim secured a position at the T. Cratchit City Hospital, which Scrooge and his cohort had helped build. In full operation for over twelve years, Tim had grown into his position with grace. He was a capable and skilled physician who cared for his patients. He worked with children. He wanted to help others get well, just as he had done.

Like Tim, Belinda yearned to care for people, and she attained a nursing position at the hospital as well. Therefore, with two Cratchit children working at the hospital, Ebenezer, Katherine, Bob, and Mrs Cratchit could not have been prouder.

With most of the children out of the house, grown and married, Bob and Mrs Cratchit had been redesigning their home. While they lived nearby, the children would come home often. Tim was the only one who still resided with his parents, as his focus on his vocation had taken precedence over anything else. Tim was all too earnest to work hard and dedicate his time to finally be called Dr Cratchit. Moreover, Bob and Mrs Cratchit quite liked that he had become a doctor, just as he imagined he would.

Tim's dearest friend, Raymond, who lived across the street, would be coming to the party with his family, along with their cousins. Mrs Cratchit had been more than happy to entertain whoever wanted to join in the celebration. The Cratchits had always been a close-knit family, but one that always welcomed friends and neighbours, especially when sharing such happy news.

Tim was dressed in his newest suit. He and Uncle Ebenezer had been outfitted together by Scrooge's tailor.

"Why you're looking quite dapper, Tim," Ebenezer said when he entered the house.

"Thank you, Uncle Ebenezer. Not so young anymore, I'm afraid."

"Ah, nor I. Everything is relative, my friend," Ebenezer said. As he'd aged, Ebenezer walked with a cane now, his bones a little more brittle, and yet his mind was still sharp. "You must feel very proud today, Tim," Ebenezer said to him as they poured some punch.

"I do feel proud, and I'm glad all of you could share in my joy."

"I believe your friend Raymond is behind me. Enjoy your party today," Ebenezer said, patting him on the back.

"I will try," Tim said, and let Ebenezer into the main room where the sounds of laughter and music filled the air.

Raymond approached the front of the house with his family and cousins in tow. Tim waved.

"Congratulations, Tim! We are so proud of you!" Raymond's mother said. Raymond shook Tim's hand and then stepped aside. "I'd like to introduce you to our cousins who are staying with us for the month. This is Nathalie and Joseph Threadstock. Nathalie and Joseph, this is Dr Timothy Cratchit."

"So wonderful to meet you," the two said, and Tim looked at Nathalie, and she at him, and something in Tim's whole demeanor changed, for it felt as if a lightning bolt had struck him right through his core, and his heart began to beat in a way it had not before.

"Please, do come in. We are so pleased you could join us," Tim said.

That day, he went on to enjoy all of his family and friends in one place, celebrating until Mrs Cratchit ran out of food, drink, and energy, and they all collapsed, exhausted from celebrating into the wee hours, feeling so pleased and happy for Tim and Belinda. And all the while, Tim could not keep his eyes off of Nathalie, nor could she keep her eyes off of him.

*

The following December, a terrible flu hit London. People were becoming ill and some were dying from it. Tim had to navigate those touchy days of caring for people and helping them to get well. He did not anticipate both Ebenezer and Lewis coming down with it for a spell.

Making house calls to them both, Tim tended to them the best that he could, while trying to protect himself, his family, and Nathalie. Lewis was not doing well. Tim was afraid for him. Ebenezer was very ill, too, but Katherine had been excellent at doting on him and trying to make him better.

When the decision came from Fred to admit Lewis to the hospital, Tim sighed with relief. Lewis did belong there. They needed to try to help him in any way that they could. Fred became worried.

*"These were some very challenging days. I was not sure if Lewis would survive the illness. Ebenezer held on for dear life, and I believe his love for Katherine sustained him. He's a stubborn one, Uncle Ebenezer, and he did not want to let her down. Plus, I just believe he has more work to do,"* Tim recounted in his journal.

In a moment of pure candour one day at the house when Ebenezer was at his lowest point, and as Katherine was making a soup, Tim sat with Uncle Ebenezer for a few moments.

"Do you believe in redemption, Tim?" Ebenezer asked.

"Of course, I do. I always have. Why do you ask?"

"Well, should this sickness take me, I am hoping that my changed nature since seeing the Ghosts will put me in good favour with You Know Who."

"You mean God?"

"That's the one."

Tim paused, then said, "I think God sees you and understands the change you have made, Uncle Ebenezer. He's a forgiving God. I don't believe he holds grudges."

Ebenezer let out a little laugh. "You see, Tim, it's conversations such as these that always make me feel better. I shall be healed in no time."

"Well," said Tim, "let's just take that one step at a time, shall we?"

Days later, both Ebenezer and Lewis were on the mend. Thanks to Tim's care, Katherine and Fred's nursing skills, and prayers sent up to God by the family, the men recovered, however a little more frail than they had been prior to getting sick.

*

One afternoon, about a year after Tim was working at the hospital, the family had set aside time for another affair. Fred, always the one to love to help out with a party, had brought in the very best food and decorations, and the small gardens in the back had been dressed for the event. Lewis, though very frail, had been able to attend with Ebenezer and Katherine, along with Fred and family and all of the Cratchits and their extended family, to see the unification of Timothy Cratchit and Nathalie Threadstock, as they married amongst their family and friends in a moment that Tim would later document as, *"...the most magical day of all of my life. To be surrounded by all those I love and those who have cared for me and been concerned for my well-being and character, I was beyond touched. Looking into my beloved Nathalie's eyes, I wanted to both cry tears of joy and shout with joy to the streets of London that at this very moment, all was right with the world."*

By spring, Tim and Nathalie held a little angel in their arms—their daughter, Simone Allison Cratchit—the spitting image of Tim as a baby, according to Mrs

Cratchit.

"She's just splendid, isn't she?" Mrs Cratchit said, holding her close to her chest and rocking her gently. "You've done well, Nathalie."

Tim and Nathalie were living in a small flat near the hospital, so that it was easy for Tim to get to work and back home again. He spent tireless hours caring for people, and the time he was able to spend with his family was precious to him. He wrote in his journal one night: *"Please don't misunderstand—I love my job as a doctor. It is everything I wanted to be with regard to a profession, but I long to be as good a dad as my own father and as good a surrogate father as Uncle Ebenezer. It's my most ardent desire to be the best father to my children."*

Of course, Tim kept that promise. Five children later, he had a big family of his own, a career as a physician, a loving wife, and extended family that grew closer thanks to the goodness Bob and Mrs Cratchit had fostered in all of them. The blending of Fred's family along with Ebenezer and Katherine, created a family that was based on love and friendship that carried them through their years, as they all looked after one another and lifted each other up.

When Ebenezer grew older and he and Katherine could no longer manage the upkeep on their large townhouse, the home went to Tim and his growing family.

"I want your family to have it now, Tim. Katherine and I don't need a place this big. We are moving into a delightful flat nearby, and I wish to see you and your family grow into this place and make it your own. Truly I do. That is my wish," Uncle Ebenezer had said.

And so that is how the journals came to be found in this old house. They clearly had been in the home for generations, but no one had ever uncovered them before. The journals had obviously been tucked away, until they were found recently when I took possession of the home after my father's passing.

While the dates are not clear on some of the pages, at some point, when Ebenezer's eyes grew tired as he aged and his fingers struggled to write, he had given the journals to Tim to keep, which Tim must have done, and he stored his own journal alongside Ebenezer's.

After all, the house had been Ebenezer Scrooge's for many, many years, until Tim and Nathalie Cratchit inherited it from Scrooge. In the end, you see, he wasn't a miser. He learned to be a giving man—a charitable man—who found a sense of family and belonging he never expected, and a sense of love. As Tim documented, "*It is difficult for me to recount all of the kindness Uncle Ebenezer has bestowed upon me. The list is too long and too great. I can only hope, if I am in the same financial position, I may be able to help others as he has. It must be so rewarding to see all the good one can do in a lifetime. Uncle Ebenezer will tell you he could have done more had he started earlier, but I said this to him recently: 'The fact is you have started, and you have helped, and continue to do so. Your generosity knows no bounds, and I, and the rest of my family, are indebted to you.'*

*To which he turned to me and said, 'No, Tim. It is I who is indebted to you.'*"

Stave Five

# The Happy End of It

Generations later, I sit in the study of this gorgeous London townhouse, the dust having settled on the renovations we made, everything put in its place. It's late at night, and my husband is sleeping soundly in our bedroom upstairs. Outside on the streets, I hear people walking, laughing, horns blowing, and the wind rustling the leaves.

Next week is Christmas. The children will be home soon to celebrate the holiday, and I'm looking forward to seeing them. I've exhausted myself combing through the journals, making sense of the scribblings and the stories. My husband says I am obsessed with the lives of Scrooge and the Cratchits, and why shouldn't I be? I am a

Cratchit. And I'm living in my great-great grandfather's home that has been passed down from generation to generation.

Oh, how I wish my father were still alive and could hear the stories that were recounted in those journals that belonged to Ebenezer and Tim. He lived in this house all that time and didn't even know that within the walls were the journals of our predecessors. Hearing their voices, written in their own hand, makes everything so much more real and the Ghosts evermore possible.

I've combed through everything at this point. I've interviewed people whose families lived in this area for generations, as well, some who have shared stories their parents and grandparents have shared with them. We keep people alive through their stories and by retelling their stories, for how can anyone truly ever be gone unless we stop talking about them? We are here to carry forward their lessons, their trials and tribulations, their loves and losses. Perhaps that is why I fancy being an historian so much. We cannot let our histories be changed for the sake of change, for they anchor us in time and place to help us understand. History is a lesson.

When you have examined the artifacts and record-
ings as I have, you may come to find out that Ebenezer
Scrooge was not a horrible person to begin with; he was
simply a grumpy man who wanted to be left alone. He
was not a people person, to put it in today's frame of ref-
erence. However, that need to be left alone and wallow in
his money and his aloneness left him inadvertently hurt-
ing people like Fred, his only nephew, who only wanted
Scrooge to be a part of his family, a part of his life. If
we, ourselves, dig deep inside our own actions and lives,
can we not say that perhaps we have done the same? Can
we not say that we have either hurt someone or pushed
someone away for reasons that may not be entirely clear?
Furthermore, have we asked those we have hurt for forgiveness or properly atoned for our own behaviors?

Fred's mother was Ebenezer's sister, and yet, he
originally found it painful to have Fred in his life because
he reminded Ebenezer of his sister. When the barrier to
the relationship was finally broken down thanks to the
unrelenting, sweet disposition of Fred, who truly wanted
nothing in return but a relationship with his uncle, everything began to change. Of course, the Ghosts helped

propel them to that point.

As well, Ebenezer understood the challenges the Cratchit family faced, and he was called to action with the nudge from the Ghosts and a desire to be a better man. He did become a second father to Tim—a second father to all the children—and like a brother to Bob and Mrs. Cratchit. They relied on him, and in the end, he relied on them. They became, for lack of a better word, family. All of them, an entangled family that was forever bonded.

I know, as most who have heard the tale know, that Scrooge did become a better person. But perhaps the most astounding aspect of reading Scrooge's journals had to be the remarkable list of his philanthropy. How many things had that man become involved with to better Old London? His smattering of good deeds is far deeper than any of us ever knew, much like uncovering da Vinci's vast collection of works. He had been party to numerous acts of kindness. And Scrooge did not want any of it publicized. He did it not for glory, but simply to help.

Scrooge did help create a reputable hospital in London for children. It was his passion. He set about finding investors with the help of his colleagues, and before long, it went from a dream to a reality. Moreover, that wasn't the only thing that came to fruition.

Learning about the dismal conditions of the orphanages, Scrooge went about trying to make them better places, and in a roundabout way, created two new orphanages that fostered love, care, and understanding. He wanted children to find permanent homes, but he knew he had to create an environment that would lead to those goals. Scrooge did that, always remembering the way he felt when his father sent him away to a boarding school when he was a child. He never wanted children to feel as desolate and alone as he had felt all those years ago.

Hand in hand with the orphanages, Scrooge and Katherine made strides to better the education system, something they were both extremely passionate about. It turns out that Katherine was not only a wonderful teacher and tutor, but also an incredibly savvy businesswoman. They persevered in building better schools and helping children of all income levels learn to read, write, and do their maths. Scrooge was impressed with her insights, and the two formed a partnership that was enviable, for it was borne of love, friendship, and understanding. They were quite a pair, and many good deeds came from it.

He also went about championing the end of the workhouses for children. Repulsed by the conditions of the workhouses and the treatment of children, Scrooge could no longer turn a blind eye to it. He began to get others in the city involved, and they formed a coalition to change that system.

On the docks, Scrooge and Faris, the butcher, leased a building whereby food donations and leftover foods could be brought and cooked for those working outside in harsh conditions. The idea of a bleak London did not appeal to Scrooge. As he documented in his journal: *"The weather here is already glum; there is no need for our citizens to feel the same way. I must do better at finding ways to make our lives more bearable...make them better. Even if I can only do the small things, those small things I shall do."*

Ebenezer Scrooge's endeavours serve to remind all of us that we do not need to do big things to make an impact. Small things count as well. A mere smile goes a long way in a world where people feel invisible. Offering someone a hand when they need it or being a good friend goes a long way. Scrooge's singular goal each day was to make people feel valued. He said so much when he wrote: *"I regret only thinking of myself, not of others. For all those years that I was caught up in my own actions, my business, and earning money, it will haunt me long after the Ghosts have left. But if I may defend myself in any of the miscues of my past life, I am thankful that I have the money to help others now. I am glad for it, for now it will be used for the common good. And if I don't have the money to do all I need to do, I will find others whose goals match my own."*

Much of the folklore about Ebenezer Scrooge paints a picture of a man who is quite elderly...near death, even. However, records show Scrooge was only fifty when the tale of the Spirits begins, and Scrooge lived a rather fulfilled life. He and Katherine grew quite old together, finding solace in each other's company and good nature. Fred, it seems, took as good care of Ebenezer and Katherine as he did of his own father, Lewis.

Dr Timothy Cratchit and his wife, Nathalie, had many children, and lived as a happy and loving family. They took great care of this home where I now live with my husband. On one wall in the house—a wall I will never touch—I found the etchings of all of Tim's children's heights scored into the wall with their names: Simone, Alexander, Henry, Elisabeth, and Sadie. There is also artwork that had been created and framed by the children that I have left hanging in the parlour. It's a charming reminder of all that had been, and their legacy lives on through their paintings and artwork.

I breathe in and look around the study that is filled with books, my eyes growing weary, the lights set to low as I continue to write and document this story.

Scrooge truly went from humbug to humble, and my family reaped the rewards of such a transformation. My fingers can't type this fast enough, and I find I'm growing steadily more tired with each word I type, my eyes becoming heavy with sleep.

*

I lift my head from the maple desk, having drifted off, and look around. The lights are dim, and I can see snow flurries outside the windows, a rare occurrence. The distant sounds of church bells and laughter from people in the streets fill the quiet air. I turn around and see a figure standing near the fireplace. I rub my eyes, trying to draw the figure into focus. He is transparent, but I can clearly make out who is before me.

In a funny looking nightshirt and robe, the figure rubs his chin and looks at me.

"Amelia, is it?"

"That's right," I say.

"Do you believe in ghosts?"

"I do, actually," I say. "I actually do."

"Good. You have no need to fear me."

"I have no fear," I say.

"This was my home, before it was Tim's, before it was yours. I was happy here."

"I know. I'm so grateful for it. I've been reading your story and Tim's in the journals."

"Ah, the journals. Ancient history, I'm afraid, but I am glad you enjoyed reading them."

"Yes," I say, looking at him. "And your story is compelling. I believe the world must know the rest of the story."

"But why, my dear? You know, and that's all that matters."

"I disagree. This is a story for all, because there is power in knowing redemption and transformation are possible. Surely, you must agree having lived it."

"I suppose I do, but I never sought recognition for the change in demeanour."

"I understand, and yet people will want to know if it's possible to change. And you, sir, serve as inspiration for those who may need to change their ways."

He pauses for a moment, pensive, wondering if it would make sense to share the rest of the story.

"May I have your permission to write this story?" I ask again.

"Truthfully, you don't need my permission."

"But it would feel so much better if I had it."

He seems to enjoy that I am seeking his approval.

"I suppose it would not hurt, only because I can sense you are one of us, Amelia. A believer."

I feel my heart become warm and I nod.

"I am one of you," I say, "and I won't let you down."

"You could never let us down, because it's all in the name of kindness. For mankind. To make the world a little better place because we were in it and wanted to leave a positive mark on it."

"Yes, and I believe my role is to share that knowledge."

"Then you shall do it," he says.

"Thank you, Ebenezer."

"You flatter me, my dear. I am humbled that you call me by my name."

"Not only I—everyone knows your name. You are a legend in these parts."

"Is that so? Well, then, I will trust you to share what you know. So, for the sake of charity and goodwill, and as a reminder of what the Christmas season is truly all about, let them know our story, dear Amelia."

"Thank you for entrusting it to me."

"It is all of our stories. And thank you. I must be off now. I hear Katherine calling for me. A very Merry Christmas to you."

The wind begins to howl, the snow swirls and collects upon the windowsill, and I gaze outside the widow. When I glance back toward the fireplace, the phantom of Ebenezer Scrooge is gone.

*

I don't know if what I have seen is a dream, a reality, or a semi-conscious waking state, but it feels as real as anything I've ever experienced before. I hunker down from that point forward and pick up where I left off with the story, attempting to tell it the best that I can.

I owe him that.

In a frenzy to get it all right, I painstakingly recount the stories that have been scribed about the lives of Scrooge and the Cratchits, feeling incredibly privileged that the story has been left in my care. Now, all I need is faith in myself that I can properly tell the rest of the story.

For all of our sakes.

# Epilogue

# Christmas Eve at Ebenezer Scrooge's House

Everyone knew Ebenezer had something up his sleeve for Christmas Day, but he did a very good job of keeping them all guessing. He'd become very secretive in the weeks leading up to the holiday. He and Katherine had decided to host Christmas Eve this year at their home. No matter how many times family and friends tried to prod him for answers, with a devilish smile on his face, he just kept saying, "I cannot tell you; it will ruin the surprise."

On Christmas Eve morning, Ebenezer left the house early to check on all the particulars for the night's gathering. Dressed in his top hat and coat, he stepped out into the winter air. Everything had been secretive, and he had asked those who were helping him with various aspects to keep a tight lip about the plans. Why, he had even gone so far as to make Ms Pishell of the Sweet Shop pledge to remain quiet about the treats he had her making for the occasion, and Ms Pischell never kept quiet about anything! As well, he had managed to do the same with the baker, the poulterer, and the trio of musicians.

Of course, Katherine was in on it, too. Inspired by the stories Ebenezer told Katherine of Old Fezziwig and his wife and the parties they had thrown when he was his apprentice, they had decided to try to replicate the fun. Katherine had been busy organizing and decorating for the last several days, making sure to bring some of the magic that Ebenezer had spoken of into their own home. They even arranged for help to create proper room for dancing in the large drawing room.

The Christmas Eve party was an opportunity for Ebenezer to give some of the joy he had received as a young man back to those he now loved and cherished. He felt sneaky, but in the best of ways.

Making his rounds, he visited Joseph Dunham, the craftsman who worked on many projects Ebenezer had been engaged in over the years. Joseph had been commissioned to create something special. When Ebenezer arrived at his shop to check on the progress, Joseph opened the door and wished him well.

"A very Merry Christmas to you, Ebenezer," he said.

"And to you! I trust you will be joining us tonight?"

"I wouldn't miss it! Come this way, I'll show you how it turned out."

Ebenezer followed Joseph into his workshop and took one look at it. "It's absolutely perfect! Excellent work, Joseph! I am indebted to you for such a fine job."

"I'm glad you like it. I'll bring it with me this evening."

"Thank you, Joseph," he said. "It will be a nice surprise."

Ebenezer paid Joseph for his work, and he found himself whistling Christmas Carols all the way home.

When Ebenezer walked through the door, Katherine and a couple of the other ladies who had also been sworn to secrecy, had finished decorating and the house looked splendid. Smelling of fresh greens and holly, ribbons were strewn from the greens, and candles were placed around the perimeter of the room. The Christmas tree Ebenezer and Katherine had decorated two nights prior stood like a beacon of hope in the middle of the room.

The guests were due to arrive at six o'clock promptly. When all the finishing touches were complete, Ebenezer and Katherine bathed and dressed for the occasion. When there was a knock at the door, Ebenezer kissed his wife and thanked her for all of her tireless help.

"It was my pleasure, darling," she said. "It will be a night to remember, and a wonderful tribute to what you learned from your former employer."

Ebenezer bounded down the stairs like a young man, albeit much stiffer than a young man, and opened the door to the musicians, who set up on the side of the room and began to play. The idea of musicians in his home excited him, and he hoped that people would take the opportunity to dance. For a moment, he wished he had learned to play the fiddle, such a lively instrument. He remembered fondly watching all of Fezziwig's friends and workers engaged in a night of celebration and levity.

Fred and his wife were first to arrive with Lewis and their children, who were now young people. Soon after, the Cratchits came through the door with their children, along with many other friends Ebenezer and Katherine had made over the years. The guests were in awe of the beauty of Ebenezer's home and how Katherine and he had transformed it into a magical Christmas Eve evening party. From the punch to the food on the table, Ebenezer played the part of the perfect host while also enjoying himself quite a bit, too! He was hopeful everyone would have a good time.

And a good time they had! The music had been a wonderful idea, and the children danced along with their parents, and their parents danced with each other, and friends danced with friends. Ebenezer marveled at how his guests knew all the latest dances, and he tried his best not to step on Katherine's toes when they attempted the Galop, the Polka, and the Viennese Waltz. If nothing else, there was uproarious laughter, and Tim and the other children tried to keep time with the music, laughing at their missteps, as well.

When the music stopped so the musicians could

take a little break, Ebenezer filled his guests' glasses. It was time for a toast. Ebenezer stepped onto the fourth step of his staircase and said, "If I may have your attention for just a brief moment, everyone."

His friends and family began to gather around to hear what he had to say.

"My dear Katherine, you must come up here beside me before I begin," and Katherine obliged. He put his arm around her and held his glass in the other. "I'm a bit out of breath from all that dancing! Can we show our musicians how much we appreciate their wonderful playing?"

All in attendance clapped and cheered for the musicians. Then, Ebenezer continued: "My friends, it is our pleasure to host you all this fine Christmas Eve. Katherine, I thank you for making the place look so spectacular and organizing the menu. You have done a tremendous job."

Everyone smiled at Katherine and applauded her. She was not much for accolades, and brushed it off, placing her head on Ebenezer's shoulder.

"As for the rest of you, we thank you for joining us

this evening. I am so genuinely happy to be connected to all of you, and you have enriched our lives beyond measure. You have made our lives happy, and we are thrilled to call you our family, our friends. Now, where is Joseph... Joseph Dunham?"

Joseph came into the room holding something draped in fabric. "Ah, there he is," Ebenezer began, as Joseph moved toward the center of the room. "Now, most of you know the wonderful craftsman, Joseph. He has helped us with lots of projects over the years, and this is one that I hope will please many of you, especially you, Bob Cratchit."

Bob looked surprised and confused at the same time. Mrs Cratchit let out a little gasp, which thoroughly pleased Ebenezer. He loved making them feel a little off kilter when he presented them with something special.

"Well, go ahead, Joseph. Unveil it!"

Joseph removed the covering and produced a handmade sign that read, "Cratchit & Cratchit."

Bob's eyes welled up.

"For many years, Scrooge & Cratchit has helped many of our friends and neighbors - both in their lives and in their businesses. None of that would have been possible without the hard work and dedication of my friend and partner Bob Cratchit. Together we have accomplished a great deal. But nothing stays the same forever. Time does indeed march on and that generally means change. But change can be good, very good. One of those good changes is that I have decided to turn the reins of the company over to Bob and his eldest, wonderful son Peter. Oh, I'll still be around here and there, but they will run the daily business operation from this day forward and its name will be Cratchit & Cratchit. With Bob's strong business sense, coupled with his kindness and good heart, I'm sure that Cratchit & Cratchit will continue to grow for many years to come, doing more and more good things to improve the lives of the fine people of London.

"Yes, I will be stepping away from Scrooge & Cratchit. But as I promised the Spirits that long-ago Christmas Eve, I will always keep Christmas in my heart. I will do this with my lovely wife and partner Katherine, giving the years we have left to helping those less fortunate in any way we can.

"Therefore, my friends, please raise a glass with me and let us toast Christmas, Cratchit & Cratchit, and life's next adventures."

"Hear, hear," they all said and raised their glasses.

"And now, let us get back to enjoying our Christmas Eve party!" Ebenezer shouted over the noise.

Bob made his way over to Ebenezer, where they shook hands, and then hugged. Peter thanked Ebenezer as well. Mrs Cratchit was crying from sheer joy, and Katherine handed her a handkerchief.

"I will not soon forget this party," Bob said to Ebenezer.

"Nor will I, Bob," Ebenezer said in return, "nor will I."

After more dancing, eating, and playing many games, at midnight Katherine and Ebenezer handed out presents to each guest in attendance that night, which was the last surprise of the evening. When they said goodbye to their last guests, Ebenezer and Katherine retired for the night and both fell fast asleep after such an eventful day.

*

On Christmas Day, Ebenezer and Katherine spent the morning at Christmas service, and then made their way to Fred's house, where the Cratchits were joining them for a more intimate celebration as they had done for many years now.

In Ebenezer Scrooge's diary, of that particular Christmas Eve and Christmas Day, he wrote the following: *"In all my life, this Christmas has been the most magical. What has taken me so long to remember what I learned from Old Fezziwig? We have the power to make other people happy, whether it's the small things or bigger things. I will cherish the memory of seeing those I love so happy, so merry. Katherine and I feel blessed to have found so much love and to be surrounded by so much love. This has been the most memorable Christmas, and I am so very thankful."*

You see, Ebenezer Scrooge did keep his promises to the Spirits. He did keep Christmas well, and he cherished the years he had left to spend with those he loved.

# THE END

# Author's Note

Charles Dickens' novella, *A Christmas Carol*, is my favorite story of all-time. I fell in love with it when I was eight years old and came in contact with the ghostly Christmas tale. A story about a person's redemption after realizing and correcting the errors of his ways continues to delight readers all these years later because the universal premise is so relatable and never goes out of fashion: Can someone truly change and become a better person?

As this story is not only my favorite, but is also beloved by my family, it led to a discussion last Christmas at the dinner table. We all wondered the following: How, exactly, did Scrooge transform? In what ways did Scrooge become a better contributor to society? Additionally, what action did Scrooge take to mend his relationships with his nephew Fred, Bob Cratchit, Tiny Tim, Isabelle, and family?

We all came up with ideas about it, and that discussion prompted me to try to fill in the blanks.

Believe me, I fear the comparisons to the one and only Charles Dickens. I humbly beg your forgiveness that I am not the great C.D. I would never want to write something that might let him down. It's true that *A Christmas Carol* is perfect the way it is; there truly is no need for a follow-up novella. However, as fan fiction is popular and writers like to try their hand at it (think Gregory Maguire and *Wicked*), I am hoping Dickens might be flattered that I gave it a shot. Nevertheless, I ask you to pardon me for filling in the blanks as I have done. Please know my heart was in the right place. Those of us in love with the happiest of endings may appreciate more backstory as to how someone as lost as Ebenezer Scrooge could turn his life around in a merry and profound way.

For these reasons, I attempted to explore the course of action Ebenezer Scrooge might have taken to put his talents and riches and kindness to work for the greater good after the three Spirits aided in his desire to transform that Christmas.

Christmas, I believe, is the most joyous time of year, and is absolutely not a humbug. Fortunately, Scrooge came to believe the same.

Wishing you a very Happy Christmas season,
*Stephanie Verni*

# Acknowledgements

Thank you to the following people for your insights and for helping to make this book happen: Jenny Bumgarner, Tom Cantilli, Chrysti Cantilli, Craig Glasheen, Barry Gogel, Elizabeth Johnson, Megan Musgrove, Doug Parrillo, Leni Parrillo, Anthony Verni, Eleanor Verni, Matthew Verni, Jo Verni, Mark Verni, and Melody Wutich.

To my editors ... *I am indebted to your for your generosity...*
To Leni Parrillo, Doug Parrillo & Anthony Verni: thank you for the painstaking job of combing through the manuscript again and again. Megan Musgrove: thank you for editing the manuscript to help make Amelia Cratchit Shannon sound British.

To my writing group and fellow scribes—Thank you for providing support and inspiration: Colleen Young, Megan Musgrove & Dana Armstrong

To my readers: I hope this makes you want to read (or go back and re-read) some of the great works of Charles Dickens, namely *A Christmas Carol.*

To my current and former students: Thank you for your support. May you always find a love of reading.

And especially to Charles Dickens: Thank you for writing something I not only fell in love with but have been obsessed with Christmas after Christmas...and all the days in between.

# About the Author
# Stephanie Verni

Ask Stephanie Verni which writer she would like to have dinner with (dead or alive), and she'll tell you it's Charles Dickens.

The author of *Beneath the Mimosa Tree, Baseball Girl, Inn Significant, Little Milestones, The Postcard,* and *Anna in Tuscany,* Stephanie enjoys writing realistic, hopeful fiction that tugs at the heart and covers themes such as forgiveness, loss, recovery, friendship, and love.

She is also the co-author of the textbook, *Event Planning: Communicating Theory and Practice.* Currently Professor of Communication at Stevenson University, she instructs writing and communication courses. She resides in Severna Park, Maryland, with her husband and two children.

Visit her website at www.stephanieverni.com.

*If you enjoyed reading this book, and during this charitable season of giving, please consider posting a review online. As indie authors, we rely upon our readers to help promote our work. From an author's standpoint, writing is our passion; the tricky part is marketing. Therefore, any help you can provide by recommending the book, sharing it on social media, or posting a review helps us continue to pursue our love of storytelling.*

Merry Christmas!

Made in the USA
Middletown, DE
17 November 2021